HAPPINESS IS A WARM BLANKET, CHARLIE BROWN™

Adapted by Jennifer Fox
Art by Paige Braddock and Vicki Scott
Cover and interior design by Frances J. Soo Ping Chow
Typography: Bembo and Typography of Coop

This special edition was printed for Kohl's Department Stores, Inc.
(for distribution on behalf of Kohl's Cares, LLC, its wholly owned subsidiary)
Published by Running Press Kids
An Imprint of Running Press Book Publishers
A Member of the Perseus Books Group
2300 Chestnut Street
Philadelphia, PA 19103-4371

Kohl's
ISBN 978-0-7624-5147-0
123386
First Edition Printed 04/13–09/13

Visit us on the web!
www.runningpress.com
www.Snoopy.com
www.Kohls.com/Cares

HAPPINESS IS
A WARM BLANKET,
CHARLIE BROWN™

BY CHARLES M. SCHULZ

RP|KIDS
PHILADELPHIA • LONDON

Linus loved his blanket. It made him feel safe and secure. It soaked up all of his fears and frustrations.

Linus didn't like to be away from his blanket ever. Not even when his sister, Lucy, decided it was time to clean it. "WASH DAY!" Lucy would shout.

"It's in the rinse cycle. . . ."
she'd say, as Linus began to sweat.

And finally,
"It's in the spin cycle."

At last, Linus would get
his blanket back.

But lately, Linus's friends had begun teasing him about his
blanket. They thought it was silly and got in the way.
"You and that stupid blanket!" Schroeder yelled.

"I can't stand it," said Charlie Brown.

Even Sally, who loved everything about Linus, had something to say about his blanket. "You're my Sweet Babboo," she told Linus. "But I could like you even more if you'd give up that blanket."

Only Charlie Brown's dog, Snoopy, understood how great
Linus's blanket really was. And *he* wanted it for himself.

Linus had an even bigger problem than teasing or a jealous dog. His grandmother was coming to visit. Gramma didn't like Linus's blanket one bit.

Lucy began to pester Linus more than ever. "If you don't give up that stupid blanket," she said, "Gramma's going to cut it into a thousand pieces!"

Linus had to find a way to give up his blanket before Gramma came. But how?

Linus tried a substitute. But that had drawbacks.

Lucy locked the blanket in a closet.
But Linus couldn't stay away.

"You'd better give it back," Charlie Brown told Lucy.
"What makes you say that, Charlie Brown?" Lucy asked.

Gramma's visit was just a few days away, and nothing seemed to work. Linus was *not* going to give up his blanket.

But someone else had other plans. . . .

"Snnoooooppppppy!!" Linus screamed.

Linus chased Snoopy everywhere. But Snoopy made a daring escape!

Seeing Linus's blanket fly through the air gave Lucy an idea.

Lucy made a kite out of Linus's blanket to keep it away from him. But Linus wasn't fooled.
"My blanket!" Linus yelled.

Things only got worse for Linus when Lucy let go of the kite. Linus watched his beloved blanket float off into the air.

Linus's blanket was really gone this time. Staring up at the great big sky, he felt sadder than he ever had. "I bet I'll never see my blanket again," he said.

Still, Linus had to try to get his blanket back. He asked Charlie Brown to help him put an ad in the paper.

"Lost. . . . One light blue blanket in the shape of a kite. . . . Please return. Owner desperate."

Even though his good friend Charlie Brown stayed by his side,
Linus could barely sleep without his blanket. He kept thinking
about it . . . wondering . . .

. . . where it could be.

Soon, Linus got some good news. It was a telegram from the Air Rescue Service.

"They found my blanket!" he told Charlie Brown. "They are mailing it back to me!"

Linus was thrilled to get his blanket back, but his happiness did not last long. Gramma was arriving that day, and Lucy had come up with a surefire way of curing Linus of his blanket habit once and for all. "I buried it," she said.

Linus dug . . .

and dug . . .

. . . and dug, but he could not find his blanket.

Just when things seemed
hopeless, Linus's blanket seemed
to find him.

It was time for Linus to face Gramma. She was not happy that Linus still had his blanket, but Linus stood his ground. "I need this blanket," he told Gramma. "It's the only real security I have."

After all, everyone had someone or something that helped them get through the day. It wasn't just Linus with his blanket.

Sally had her
"Sweet Babboo," Linus.

Schroeder had his piano.
Lucy had Schroeder.

Snoopy had his dinner bowl.

Even Gramma had her coffee.

Linus made a good argument for keeping his blanket, but Gramma would not listen. "Hand it over?" Linus asked. "You want me to hand it over?"

Sure enough, Gramma took Linus's blanket away.

But Gramma didn't really get Linus's blanket. He had swapped it with a dish towel, and tricked her. After Gramma had gone, Linus got out his real blanket.

Charlie Brown was happy for Linus. Everything was back to normal, and Linus's blanket was safe. Still, Linus was a little sad to see Gramma go.

"I'm going to miss the thrill of the chase," he told Charlie Brown.

Luckily for Linus, *someone* would always want his blanket.